Patches
Lost and Found

Steven Kroll • Illustrated by Barry Gott

Marshall Cavendish
New York   London   Singapore

J enny loved to draw pictures.
 She drew pictures of Mom and herself on vacation.
 She drew pictures of her house and the street
where they lived.
 She drew pictures of her pet guinea pig, Patches.
 She drew pictures of her school and her teacher,
Mr. Griswold.

One Monday, Mr. Griswold announced to the class: "Your assignment for next Monday is to write a story. You can work on it at school and at home."

"Could I draw a picture instead?" Jenny asked.

Mr. Griswold shook his head. "Not unless it goes with the words. Words first!"

All the way home on the school bus, Jenny tried to think of something to write about. Nothing came. Her mind was like an empty sack. Writing had always been hard for her.

When she got home, Mom asked, "How was school?"

"Not so good," said Jenny. "I have to write a story."

"I want to hear more about it," said Mom, "but first, I have to tell you, Patches is missing! I went to feed him, and his cage door was open!"

"Oh, no!" said Jenny. "My poor guinea pig!"

"Let's look for him," Mom said. "He must be nearby."

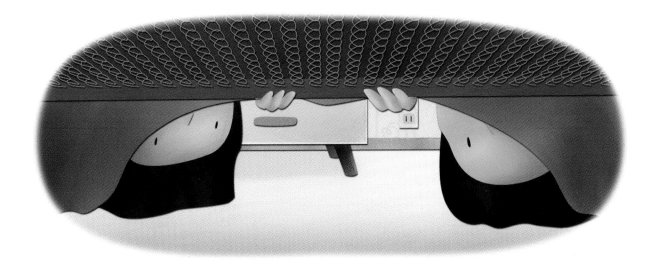

They looked under Jenny's bed and in her
closet. They looked in Mom's room and all over
the house.
NO PATCHES!

"I have an idea," Mom said. "Why don't you make some posters? We'll put them up around the neighborhood."

"Okay," said Jenny.

She pulled out paper and crayons and drew a picture of a big white guinea pig. He had a black patch over one eye and another over his tail. Under the picture, she wrote PATCHES and LOST and her phone number.

After dinner, Jenny and her mom put up the posters.
But by bedtime, there was still no Patches.
The next morning, he hadn't shown up either.
   "Where could he be?" Jenny asked at breakfast.
   "I'm sure he'll turn up," answered Mom.

Jenny went back to her room. She sketched what could have happened to Patches. She drew him skittering out the back door. Then she drew him hiding under a bush in the garden. She taped the drawings to her wall.

They hadn't looked in the garden. Maybe
Patches was there. Jenny went out to check, but
he wasn't under any bushes.

At school, Jason and Allison asked Jenny, "Have you thought of a story yet?"

"No," said Jenny miserably. "I haven't thought of anything."

When Jenny got home that afternoon, she raced into her mom's office.

"Sorry, Jenny, still no Patches," Mom said.

Jenny pulled out paper and crayons. She drew more pictures about what could have happened. She drew a picture of a thief stealing Patches and running down the street. Then she drew another picture of the thief getting on a motorcycle and riding away.

She taped both pictures to the wall.

Wednesday came and went. No word on Patches, and Jenny still didn't have an idea for her story.

"Any progress?" Mr. Griswold asked.

Jenny shook her head.

At home that night, Jenny finished more drawings. She drew the thief carrying Patches onto a train. She drew a passenger on the train spying the thief and calling the police.

She hung both pictures on the wall.

On Thursday, Jenny asked Mom if she could stay home from school. She hadn't thought of a story, and she hadn't found Patches.

"Okay," said Mom. "You do look pale. Maybe a day of rest will do you good."

Jenny stayed in her room. She drew a picture of the police setting out to capture the thief. She drew another of the police arresting him.

She taped both pictures to her wall.

On Friday, Jenny really did feel sick. She had a sore throat and a cough. All day long, she drew more pictures.

She drew the police taking the thief off to jail. She drew the police captain carrying Patches home to her and her family. She drew a picture of herself and Mom standing in their doorway welcoming Patches home.

She taped all three pictures to her wall.

The next day was Saturday, and Jenny didn't have to worry about going to school. As she was finishing breakfast, someone knocked on the door.

Mom went to open it.

"Hi," said Mr. Scooter from down the block. "I think I have something for you."

He blinked through his thick glasses. In his arms was Patches.

"Patches!" Jenny shouted. "Where did you find him, Mr. Scooter?"

"Under a bush. I didn't see your posters until last night. By then, he'd nibbled my whole lawn. Better than any lawnmower."

"Oh, my goodness," said Mom.

"Oh, thank goodness," said Jenny.

She gave Patches a hug and a squeeze.

Later that day, Mom came into Jenny's room. Jenny was cuddling Patches.

"So what are you going to write your story about?"

Jenny shrugged. "I can't think of anything."

Mom glanced up. "Look at all these pictures. They tell a wonderful story! All you have to do is add words to your pictures."

Mom was right. Jenny found it was easy to add words now that she had done all the pictures.

Once upon a time Patches escaped from his cage and ran outside.

Outside was scary. Patches hid under a bush.

A big bad mean old thief came and stole him.

The thief stuck Patches in his pock and rode away on h motorcycle. "Squeak! Squeak cried Patches

"Shut up!" yelled the big bad mean old thief. He jumped onto a train.

Patches kept squeaking. The thief couldn't keep him quiet. A passenger saw them and called the police.

The police leaped into their car and raced after the train.

They climbed onboard. "Stick 'em up!" they yelled as they arrested the big bad mean old thief.

They drove him to jail, and he confessed.

The Police Captain took Patches back to Jenny and her family.

They were so happy to see him. "Welcome home, Patches!"

On Monday, Jenny brought her story, PATCHES LOST AND FOUND, to school. She read it out loud to her class.

"Your story's great!" said Allison.

"Congratulations!" said Jason.

"Nice job," said Mr. Griswold. "Words first, pictures second."

"No," said Jenny. "Pictures first, words second."

"You mean you did all the pictures first?" said Mr. Griswold.

"Yes!" said Jenny.

"Well," said Mr. Griswold. "You've taught me something. I'd like to meet Patches. Why don't you bring him to school?"

For Kathleen
—S.K.

For Rose and Finn
—B.G.

Marshall Cavendish, 99 White Plains Road, Tarrytown, NY, 10591
www.marshallcavendish.us

Library of Congress Cataloging-in-Publication Data
Kroll, Steven.
Patches lost and found / by Steven Kroll; illustrated by Barry Gott. —1st Marshall Cavendish paperback ed.
p.   cm.
Summary: Jenny draws, then writes, a story about losing and finding her pet guinea pig.
ISBN: 0-7614-5217-6
[1. Lost and found possessions—Fiction. 2. Guinea pigs—Fiction.
3. Drawing—Fiction. 4. Authorship—Fiction. 5. Schools—Fiction.] I. Gott, Barry, ill. II. Title.

PZ7.K9225 Par 2005
[E]—dc22   2004058489

Creative Director: Bretton Clark
Designer: Billy Kelly
Editor: Margery Cuyler

The illustrations in this book were prepared digitally.
Printed in Malaysia
First Marshall Cavendish paperback edition, 2005
Reprinted by arrangement with WinslowHouse International, Inc.

2 4 6 8 10 9 7 5 3 1